Sherman and the Sheep Shape Contest

Story by Harriet Zaidman

Illustrations by Sonia Nadeau

Peanut Butter Press

Peanut Butter Press
9-1060 Dakota Street
Winnipeg, MB R2N 1P2

The artwork in this book was rendered in watercolour.
The text is set in 13 pt Chalkduster.

Book design by Melanie Matheson, Blue Claw Studio.
Printed and bound in Hong Kong
by Paramount Printing Company Limited/Book Art Inc., Ontario, Canada.

This book is Smyth sewn casebound.

10 9 8 7 6 5 4 3 2 1

LIBRARY AND ARCHIVES CANADA CATALOGUING IN PUBLICATION

Zaidman, Harriet, 1952-, author
Sherman and the Sheep Shape Contest / written by Harriet Zaidman ; illustrated by Sonia Nadeau.

ISBN 978-1-927735-05-3 (bound)

I. Nadeau, Sonia, 1974-, illustrator II. Title.

PS8649.A382S54 2014   jC813'.6   C2014-905826-8

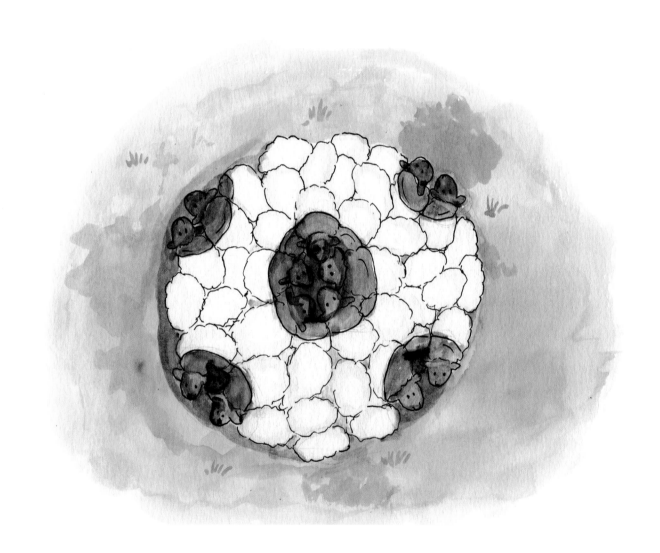

The sun smiled across the sky. Wispy clouds floated on summer breezes.

Down in the pasture, though, it was anything but calm. Songbirds trembled in their nests and gophers scurried into their tunnels. The wide-eyed sheep bumped and jostled each other as Barney, the Border collie, circled them. He barked commands and nipped at their hooves. They bleated loudly.

Sherman skidded to a stop, uttering a plaintive "BAAA".

The first Sheep Shape Contest ever held in the valley was only one week away. All the sheep on the farms were practising for the competition, but at Shear Haven Farm, neither Sherman nor any of his friends could find their places.

The farmer whistled and Barney veered away. Heaving a sigh, the farmer took off his hat and squinted at the instruction sheet. He sank down against a tree trunk. A moment later he was snoring. The paper in his hand fluttered in the wind.

Barney flopped down beside him. The sun's rays lulled the dog into dozing, his paws twitching as he dreamed.

Sherman's friends continued bleating.
He wandered near the fence, hoping for a
moment of quiet.

He leaned on the gate. Its hinges creaked
and the gate swung open.

Sherman's heart thumped as he scampered
through the opening and down the road,
escaping the din and dust of the pasture.

His friends, busy bleating, didn't notice.

Sherman trotted along until he found himself on the edge of a town. He heard sounds that frightened him at first, but then he came upon a playground. Laughing children flew back and forth on swings and clambered over a play structure.

Their cheerful chatter eased his worries. He joined the queue of children slipping down the slide. He added his bleats to their hoots and hollers.

A clanging bell interrupted their fun.

"Line up," the teacher called. Sherman got into step as the teacher shepherded her flock into the classroom.

Sherman sat at a front row desk, his hooves folded, eager for more fun. But when the class got down to work, his head began to throb.

He could only write 'BAA' for each word on the spelling test. He couldn't find a box for 'grass' as a choice on the sheet of healthy food words. And at the whiteboard, the kids complained when his fleece erased their work.

It was time for math. The class was learning to form groups. The children jumped up from their desks and Sherman did, too. The teacher called out numbers and the children dashed around, merging and dividing into groups of 2, 3, 4 and 5.

"Excuse me," Alice said, stepping around him.

"Whoa—my mistake," Georgia said, sending him sideways.

Sherman tried to join in, but he collided with a desk. The teacher had to help him untangle his legs from around a chair. He felt too muddled to bleat his confusion and could only watch.

The recess bell brought him relief. He tumbled out of the school, dizzy and dog-tired. Pining for the pasture and his friends, he started for the road, but Alice caught up with him.

"Don't leave," she said, fitting a blue vest over his head. "You can be on our team." She scribbled a note on her clipboard, ruffled his curls and hurried to her spot on the sidelines.

A whistle blew, followed by a thundering noise. Startled, Sherman saw a wall of red-vested players headed his way, charging after a black and white ball.

"Come on," Georgia shouted to Sherman as the ball flew past.

The soccer game was on.

Sherman's team tried hard, but the red team scored early and controlled the play. A blue player finally got a lucky break and booted the ball past the red goalie, evening the score at 1-1. Some spectators groaned, some cheered.

Before they knew it, the timekeeper shouted, "Two minutes left!"

The red team snagged the ball and surged up the field. The blue players chased helplessly.

Sherman stopped short.

"One minute!" came the voice. A shot by the red team went wide, bringing the play to a halt.

Sherman looked around. Remembering the lesson in math, he went into action.

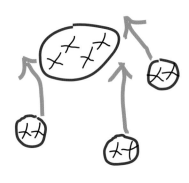

He nudged Georgia against a teammate and crowded them both against another blue player.

"Hey!" Georgia yelled. Sherman ran a circle around them. "What's going on?"

"BAAA," Sherman bleated. He herded the children toward the ball. "BAAA."

Alice rushed over. "Why—?" she asked. Then her eyes lit up. "Oh, I see. Time out!" She waved her team into a huddle around Sherman.

"Make groups," she said. "Like in math class." Alice drew circles and arrows on her clipboard. "Forwards, we need a group of four in the centre. Midfielders, divide into twos on the sides. Defence, pair up in the middle."

Sherman baaed his approval.

Georgia gave him a squeeze and rubbed his ears. "You're the best," she said. Their team got into position on the field.

Sherman ran faster than he ever had in the pasture. He and his teammates hoofed the ball from one group to the other. Everything seemed to be going according to plan until a red player stole the ball. The crowd began the countdown—10, 9, 8—

The blue midfielders kept their cool and intercepted. Working together, they passed the ball—7, 6, 5, 4—

Sherman got possession. With the goal in sight and the red defenders advancing, he used his head and butted the ball. It soared high in the air, over the defenders—3, 2, 1—the red goalie lunged, but the ball zoomed past him and through the posts, just as the bell signalled the end of recess.

"BAAA," Sherman bleated. "BAAA."

The spectators poured onto the field to congratulate him, but Sherman swerved and ran—out of the schoolyard and down the road.

"Wait!" The children rushed after him. "Wait for us."

"Children!" the teacher called when she saw her students running away from school. She trailed after them.

Sherman sprinted all the way back to Shear Haven, the kids and the teacher at his heels. Barney and the farmer were surprised to see the unusual gang invading the pasture. The kids laughed to see so many sheep, while the teacher gasped for breath. Barney barked and Sherman's friends baaed their greetings.

Sherman nipped the instructions for the sheep shape from the farmer's hand.

"Hey!" the farmer said. "What's going on?"

Sherman thrust the paper at Georgia and Alice. They twisted it about, studying the directions.

"Do you want...?" Georgia asked, looking at Sherman. He waggled his blue vest and bleated.

"Yes, of course." Alice turned to the farmer. "He wants you to put the sheep into groups," she told him. "Then arrange the groups into the shape."

"That's right," the teacher exclaimed. "Well done, Alice and Georgia." She raised her arms and announced, "It's outdoor education, children. Let's help these sheep get into shape!"

The kids whooped with joy. They took off their vests, clipping them around the sheep's fleecy bellies. The farmer taught Barney new whistles. The dog wagged his tail and went to work. This time he yipped and yapped, encouraging them into groups of 2, 3, 4 and 5, guiding them into different combinations.

The sheep bumped and jostled each other at first. But by the time the final school bell rang in town, the kids, the dog, the sheep and the adults were all exhausted, but happy.

A week later the flock assembled in perfect formation at Barney's commands. The mayor and the town councillors made speeches applauding their accomplishments and awarded them First Prize in the Sheep Shape Contest. All the sheep wore their medals with pride. The farmer nailed his to the fence for passers-by to admire.

From then on the children and the teacher got fresh air and exercise by jogging out to the farm. The kids taught the sheep how to play soccer, and Sherman helped them figure out their math problems. Barney kept everyone organized. The teacher kept track of their progress on her new clipboard.

It wasn't long before the kids and the sheep advanced to complex equations, and the farmer designed elaborate new sheep shapes for future contests.

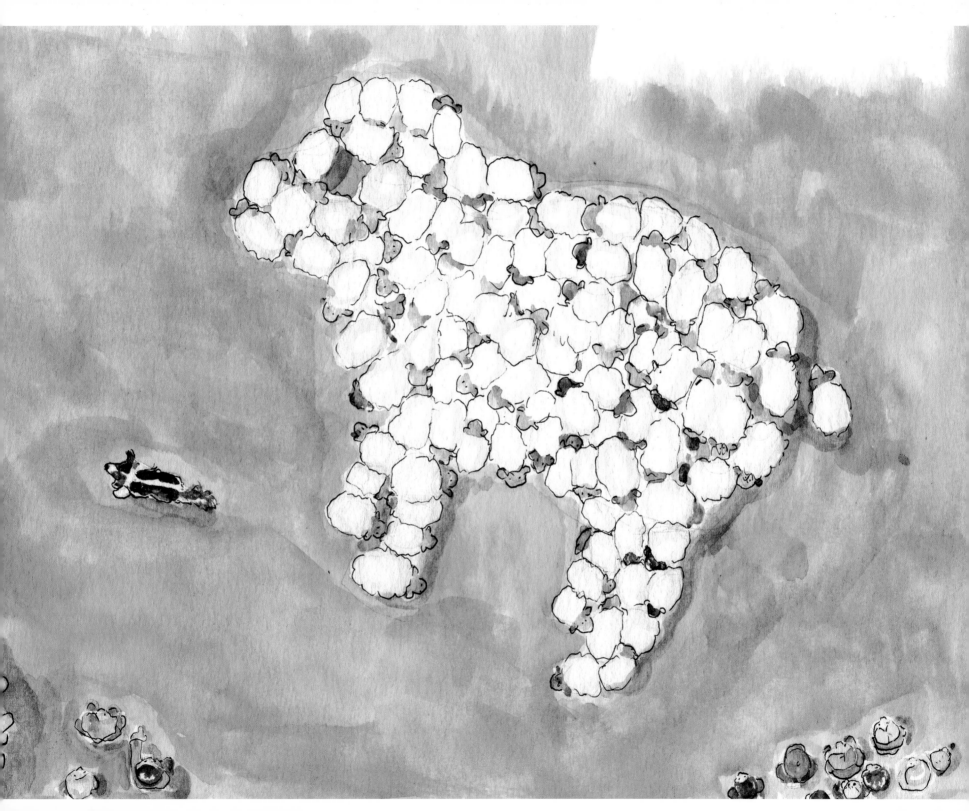

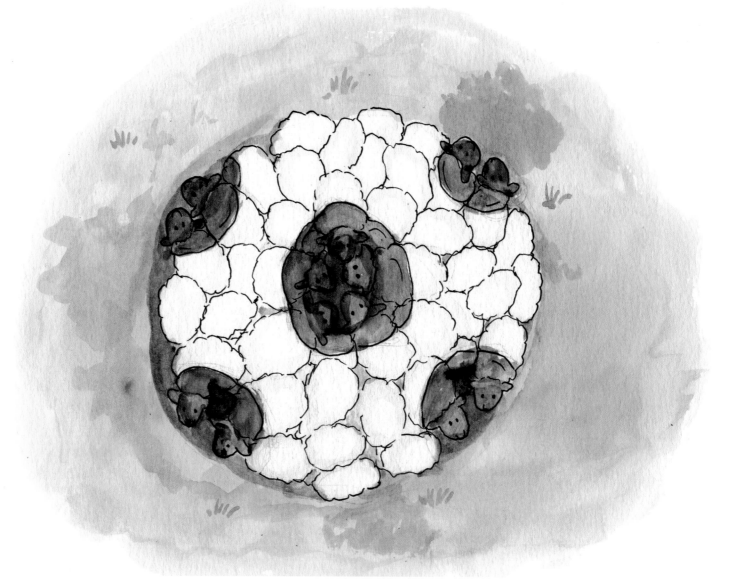

The sun beamed across the sky. Down in
the pasture songbirds trilled and gophers
squeaked their support as the teams practised
their skills and polished their drills.

"Baa," Sherman bleated contentedly. "Baa."